Dress Rehearsal

Annie K. darted out from behind the tree.

"Ra-ta-tu-ee!" cried Olmo. "You are an evil, mad duchess from outer space."

Annie glared at him. "Out of my way, you old-fashioned string-bean lizard!" Suddenly Annie felt a tapping on her shoulder. It was Gregory.

"What do you want?" Annie said. "You're interrupting our play."

"There's someone out there," Gregory said softly. "There's someone watching us."

Annie looked at the edge of the circle. Someone was sitting on the ground watching them. Someone she'd never seen before.

It was the audience!

Other Bantam Skylark Books you will enjoy
Ask your bookseller for books you have missed

Annie K.'s Theater

The Dinosaur Tooth

by
Sharon Dennis Wyeth

With illustrations by
Heidi Petach

A BANTAM SKYLARK BOOK®
NEW YORK · TORONTO · LONDON · SYDNEY · AUCKLAND

RL 3, 007–010

THE DINOSAUR TOOTH
A Bantam Skylark Book / August 1990

*Skylark Books is a registered trademark of Bantam Books, a division
of Bantam Doubleday Dell Publishing Group, Inc. Registered in
U.S. Patent and Trademark Office and elsewhere.*

ISBN 0-553-15815-5

Published simultaneously in the United States and Canada

Bantam Books are published by Bantam Books, a division of Bantam Doubleday Dell Publishing Group, Inc. Its trademark, consisting of the words
"Bantam Books" and the portrayal of a rooster, is Registered in U.S. Patent
and Trademark Office and in other countries. Marca Registráda. Bantam
Books, 666 Fifth Avenue, New York, New York 10103.

PRINTED IN THE UNITED STATES OF AMERICA

CWO 0 9 8 7 6 5 4 3 2 1

For
Annie Koehne, Gregory Dennis,
Rebecca Richardson,
Olmo Tighe, and Georgia Wyeth

Chapter One

The New Boy

"I've thought up a play," said Annie Kramer to her friend Becca. "It's a play about the very last dinosaur. And *we're* going to put it on."

Annie and Becca were sitting in their secret spot, which they called their hideout. Becca plucked a dandelion. "How many people are in it?"

"Four," said Annie, counting on her fingers.

"How can you put on a play with four people," said Becca, "when there are only two of us?"

Annie looked at the red-brick house that

1

stood a short distance from the hideout. The house was right next to her own. Her best friend Nancy McBride had once lived there.

"I wish Nancy hadn't moved," Annie said sadly. "If she were here, she would be in my play."

"What was that?" Becca said suddenly.

"What was what?" said Annie.

"I heard a noise," said Becca. "It sounded like tapping."

Annie sat down on a tree stump. "It's probably the new kid," she said. "The one who lives in Nancy McBride's house."

"It's not Nancy's house anymore," Becca reminded her. "Nancy moved at the beginning of the summer. Listen!" she said. "I hear it again."

Annie listened to the sound for a moment. Then she looked through the trees at the red-brick house. "It *is* the new kid," she said, pointing to an upstairs window. "Look."

Becca looked up at the window. A boy's thin face peeked down at them and then disappeared. "I wonder what he was tapping with," Becca said.

"Probably some kind of toy," said Annie. The new boy looked younger than she was. Becca was younger, too. Now that Nancy had moved, Annie was the only one on the block who was nine.

"Why doesn't he come outside?" Becca wondered.

"I don't know," Annie said. "I waved at him once, but he didn't wave back."

Becca took her shoes off. "Maybe he's afraid of poison ivy. Let's tell him there's no poison ivy in the hideout."

The hideout was a large, grassy circle at the end of the girls' road. It was called a hideout because it was hidden by a curtain of shade trees. In one of the trees, a small treehouse had been built on some low branches. In another hung an old tire swing. Beyond the circle were the woods of a nature preserve. The house closest to the hideout, the one with green shutters, was where Annie lived.

"You could have him be in your play," suggested Becca.

Annie looked at the red-brick house again. The boy had not come back to the window.

"No," she said. "I don't think he'd like to. I think he's shy."

Becca got up. "Let's put on a fairy tale. How about Snow White and Rose Red?"

"Nope," said Annie. "That's for babies. How about Nancy McBride moves to Japan? You'll be Nancy, and I'll be the airline pilot."

Becca shook her head. "We did that yesterday."

"All right," said Annie. "How about Nancy McBride goes to the beach? You can be Nancy, and I'll come visit you!"

"I'm tired of pretending to be Nancy McBride," Becca said. "Maybe I'll go home and read."

"Don't do that," said Annie. Nancy had been her first best friend, but Becca was a best friend also. "How about playing witches?" she suggested, picking something she knew that Becca would like.

"Great!" said Becca. "I'll get the capes!" She ran over to the treehouse.

"Hurry," said Annie. "I'll get Bomber!" She ran across the grassy circle to her house.

4

Bomber, Annie's black cat, was sunning herself on the porch.

"Hey, Bombs," Annie said, scooping up her pet. "I'm a witch and you're my familiar!" Bomber blinked and then stretched. She kneaded her paws against Annie.

"What's a familiar?" Becca called from the treehouse.

"That's what a witch calls her animal best friend," Annie explained. "I read it in the encyclopedia when I looked up the word witch. A bat is a witch's familiar also."

"Here are our capes!" yelled Becca. Two navy blue bedspreads came fluttering down.

Bomber leapt up and dive-bombed the costumes.

Annie giggled and yanked the bedspreads away. "Hey, stop that, Bomber! You're supposed to be our familiar, not tear up our witch capes." She wrapped one of the spreads around her shoulders. "I'm Warty Witch," she said to Becca.

"And," Becca said, putting on the other cape, "I'll be Burpy Witch."

Something small and dark soared over their heads and landed right in the middle of the circle.

"What's that?" said Annie. She pushed her blond bangs out of her eyes and looked at the object closely.

"It looks like a bird made out of wire and paper," said Becca.

"It's a bat," a boy's voice said.

Annie and Becca looked over their shoulders. A boy with large, dark eyes and curly, black hair was peeking out from behind a pine tree. It was the new boy.

"Hi," said Annie. "My name is Annie Kramer. In school they call me Annie K."

The boy stepped out all the way. "Hi," he said very softly.

The boy was short and thin. He looks even younger than Becca, Annie thought.

"Hi, there," said Becca. A friendly grin flashed across her round face. "My name is Becca."

"My name is Gregory," the boy said as he walked over and picked up the bat. "A bat is a witch's familiar."

Annie smiled. "Hey, that's right! Just like cats are! How did you know that?"

Gregory looked down at his sneakers. "I heard you say it."

"I saw you watching us from your window," said Annie.

"We heard you making a tapping noise," said Becca.

"What were you tapping with?" Annie asked.

Gregory picked up the bat. "This. I made it. I was testing its wings."

"Do you want to play with us?" Becca asked.

"We're about to play witches," said Annie. "When we play witches, we usually fly around, and then we have a witch picnic. Today we're having stuffed caterpillars and rotten acorns."

Gregory looked puzzled.

"Of course," Becca said, "it's only pretend. You don't have to eat anything. And you won't have to be a witch. You could be the wizard."

Gregory stared at his sneakers. "Could I be . . . a bat?"

"Sure," Annie said. "Get behind Becca. We're going to pretend that we're flying!"

Annie and Becca raced off through the trees. Their capes flapped in the wind. Bomber tore off behind them.

"Whoosh!" yelled Annie.

"We're off to the moon!" cried Becca.

Making a humming noise, Gregory followed, holding his bat.

"Good flying," Annie said to Gregory. Maybe the new boy wasn't so shy after all, she thought.

"Annie! Annie, where are you?" a woman's voice called. "That's my mom," said Annie, dropping her cape. She left the grassy circle and came back with three shiny green apples.

"Mom knows Becca and I get kind of hungry," she explained. "Gregory, here's one for you."

Gregory shook his head. "No, thank you."

"It's okay," Annie said, shoving an apple into his hand. "You don't have to act shy around us."

Gregory handed the apple back. "No, thank you. I can't."

9

"Do you have allergies?" Becca asked.

Gregory smiled. "No, I have a loose tooth." He pointed to one of his front teeth.

"You *should* eat an apple," said Annie. "That will make your tooth come right out."

"I don't want it to," Gregory said.

"What's wrong?" said Annie. "Don't you want to get money from the tooth fairy?"

"Sure, I do," said Gregory, "but not until my tooth falls out by itself."

"I know what you mean," Becca said kindly. "It'll hurt if you pull it."

Gregory lowered his eyes. Then he picked up his bat and walked away.

"Hey!" said Annie. "Where are you going? I wanted to ask you something. Since you liked playing witches, I thought you might want to—"

"Sorry," said Gregory. "I have to go inside."

"Well, when are you coming back out?" yelled Annie.

Gregory didn't turn around. "I don't know." He called over his shoulder, "Maybe tomorrow." And as quietly as he'd slipped outside, he slipped back in.

Dino Talk

"Reech-ra, reech-ra, patoot!" Annie said to Becca. "How does that sound?"

It was the next day and the two girls were up in the treehouse. Annie had a pencil and notebook. She was writing down lines for her play.

"Reech-ra, reech-ra, patoot," repeated Becca. "What does it mean?"

"It's dinosaur talk," said Annie, putting down her notebook. "It's for the play."

"Reech-ra, reech-ra," Becca said, looking down from the tree. "Here comes Gregory and he's got someone with him."

"Good!" exclaimed Annie, dangling her legs out the treehouse door. "Now we can have a rehearsal!"

"Have you finished the whole play?" Becca asked as the two of them climbed down the ladder.

"Not really," said Annie. "But I've got enough for us to get started."

She walked over to meet Gregory.

"Hi," said Annie.

"Hi," said Gregory.

"Who's your friend?" Annie asked.

"This is Olmo," Gregory said. He pointed to the boy standing next to him. He was a bit taller than Gregory, with curly, red hair and bright blue eyes.

"Hi, I—I'm Olmo," the boy said, grinning.

Annie smiled at him. There was something about the boy that was funny. Funny in a very nice way. She liked him. "I'm putting on a play about dinosaurs this afternoon," she told him. "Gregory's going to be in it."

"I am?" said Gregory.

"Yes," said Annie. "I was going to ask you. Now, Olmo can be in it, too. Okay?"

"I don't know," said Gregory. "We were going to play marbles."

Olmo took a bag out of his pocket. "That's right. We're going to play marbles!"

"Marbles!" said Becca, running over. "Can *I* play?"

"Wait a minute!" said Annie. "What about the play? Marbles is so boring."

"Maybe we can rehearse the dino play after we play marbles," Becca suggested.

"I want to do it now," insisted Annie.

The voice of Mr. Kramer calling interrupted them.

"We're here, Dad," Annie called back.

Annie's father appeared at the edge of the circle, holding a large bowl of grapes. "I thought you and your friends might be hungry," he said, waving at Becca, Gregory, and Olmo.

"Hi, Mr. K.!" Becca called brightly.

"Thanks a lot, Dad," Annie said. She took the bowl and walked back to her friends. Olmo leapt at the grapes. "Oh, boy!" he said. "I'm starved!"

"Me, too," said Becca, walking over.

"Not so fast," Annie said, snatching the bowl away. "These are for later."

"Why can't we have them now?" Becca wanted to know.

"They're props," Annie said slyly. "The grapes are dino food for my play. Only dinosaurs get to eat them."

"Okay, okay," said Olmo. "Let's put on your play. I'm hungry."

"Me, too," said Becca. "I'm not too good at marbles anyway."

Annie looked at Gregory. "What about you?"

"Okay," Gregory agreed. "Since nobody else wants to play marbles."

"All right, everyone," Annie directed, getting excited. "All three of you are going to be dinosaurs. And I'll play the part of the narrator."

Olmo did a cartwheel. "Can we eat the grapes now?"

"In a minute," Annie said. "Stand still. You'll be the father."

"What are we?" asked Becca.

14

"You and Gregory are the baby dinosaurs," explained Annie. "Get on the ground."

"I don't want to be a baby," said Gregory.

"Okay," said Annie. "You can be an egg then. That's even better. First you and Becca will be eggs, and then you'll get born."

Becca looked puzzled. "How do we do that?"

"Just curl up on the ground and pretend you're hatching," said Annie. "Then the father dinosaur will say his line and come and feed you some grapes."

"What's my line?" Olmo said, giving the air a karate chop.

"You'll say, 'I'm King Tyrannosaurus Rex! I have come to take my children!'" Annie told him. "Then you'll feed the babies some grapes."

"I can't eat grapes," interrupted Gregory, "because of my tooth."

"When your tooth finally does fall out, you're going to be rich," said Olmo. "The longer a tooth takes to fall out, the more money you get. You'll probably get five dollars!"

15

"Five dollars!" said Gregory. "I could buy a lot with that."

"I only get fifty cents for my teeth," said Becca.

"Will you please stop talking about teeth!" said Annie impatiently. "We're supposed to be rehearsing the play."

"Okay," said Becca, curling up on the ground again.

"I'm ready," said Gregory, curling up beside her.

Annie took her place as the narrator. "Once upon a time," she said in a loud voice, "there were two dino eggs in the mud. They were the children of the very last dinosaur."

Annie poked Becca and Gregory gently. "Go ahead and hatch!" she whispered.

Becca and Gregory wiggled around on the ground.

"Then," Annie continued in a booming voice, "their father came to feed them and take them away. He knew that they were in danger." Annie looked over at the pine tree. "Hey, where's Olmo?" she said in her regular voice.

Gregory pointed up to the sky.

Becca giggled. "Up in the treehouse."

Annie looked at the treehouse. Olmo had climbed up there with some grapes.

"Olmo," she scolded, "what are you doing?"

"I am tyra—tyra—tyra . . . I can't say that word," he said, blushing.

"Okay," said Annie. "Just say Rex then."

Olmo stuffed some grapes into his mouth. He stood up in the doorway of the treehouse, then swung onto a limb.

"I am Rex!" he yelled loudly. "I have come to take my children! They are in danger! I will save them from the mad duchess!" He jumped down onto the ground and grabbed some more grapes.

"Wow!" said Annie, impressed with Olmo's loud voice and gymnastic skill. "That was good. Who's the mad duchess?"

"The mad duchess is from outer space," Olmo explained with his mouth full. "She's the one who killed all the dinosaurs."

Annie stared at him. "Who told you that?"

"Nobody," said Olmo. "I just thought of it."

"But this is *my* play," Annie objected. "I was

17

going to have the dinosaurs killed by a flood."

"I think being killed by a mad duchess from outer space sounds better," Gregory piped up.

"And you could play the part of the mad duchess," Becca told Annie, getting excited.

"Yes, maybe I could," Annie said, thinking it over. "I could play two parts. The mad duchess and the narrator. Thanks, Olmo. That's a good idea."

"I have an idea, too," said Becca. "We could make the play into a fairy tale. Fairy tales make the very best plays."

"Not necessarily," said Annie. "This play is not a fairy tale."

"It could be," said Becca. "The dinos could be a prince and princess under a spell."

"I'll think about it," Annie said, trying to be patient.

"What I want to know is how it's going to end," Gregory said.

"I don't know," said Annie. "I haven't decided yet."

"I know!" said Olmo. He spun around until he was dizzy. "The mad duchess comes down and fights Rex. And all the dinos defeat her."

"How?" said Annie.

Olmo stood still for a moment. "With spit balls!"

Gregory giggled and Becca giggled and then Annie joined in.

"Reech-ra! Reech-ra!" Becca cried, pointing to the grape bowl.

"What's that mean?" said Gregory.

"It's dino talk," Becca said. "It means Olmo ate all the grapes!"

Annie picked up her notebook. "Leave me alone for a minute," she told them. "I have to think."

She sat down on the ground and began to scribble. It was going to be a very good play, she thought. That is . . . if Olmo could learn to stand still and say tyrannosaurus and Becca would stop thinking about fairy tales and Gregory would stop thinking about his tooth and leave his marbles at home and if Annie's mother would buy a huge supply of grapes and if they could get an audience . . .

Then it would be a very good play.

The Audience

Two days later, Annie had finished writing the dinosaur play and she and Becca had also finished the costumes.

"Here they are!" Annie announced to Olmo and Gregory as she and Becca came down off Annie's porch. Becca was carrying two painted boxes with eyeholes. Annie was carrying a third one.

"Aren't they good!" Becca said. "They're dino heads!"

"Great!" said Olmo. "I'll take this one." He reached out and grabbed one from Becca.

"Watch it!" said Annie. "They're still wet!"

"I'll be careful," Olmo said, putting it on.

Becca giggled. "You look good in it." The four of them crossed over into the hideout.

"This one is for you," Annie said, turning to Gregory.

"What is it?" asked Gregory, staring at the small green box she was holding.

"It's a triceratops," replied Annie. "See, I glued on three horns. Becca's is a triceratops also."

"I don't like wearing masks," Gregory said.

"It's not a mask," said Annie. "Try it on."

Gregory held the box very carefully by the edges and put it on.

"Wow!" said Becca. "That looks great!"

"Merry momerwol," Olmo agreed.

"What did you say?" Annie asked him.

Olmo took off his head. "Very wonderful," he repeated.

Annie gave him a pleased smile. "Now, all three of you try them on together," she directed.

Olmo and Becca put on their dino heads, and Gregory kept his on.

"They are wonderful," Annie agreed. "I'm so glad because today's our first dress rehearsal," she added. "And this afternoon we'll put on the play in front of an audience."

"Wow!" said Becca. "An audience!"

"I don't want one," Gregory said quietly.

"But having an audience is part of putting on a play," Annie argued.

"Why?" said Gregory.

"Because—because . . . we have to have somebody to watch us," Annie said.

Gregory looked down at his sneakers. He put his hands behind his back. He didn't say anything.

"Maybe Gregory is right," Becca said in a sympathetic voice. "Maybe we don't need an audience."

"That's ridiculous," said Annie. "We *do*!"

Just then she caught sight of Olmo. He was dangling the head in front of Bomber's face. The cat was jumping up and down and trying to scratch it.

"Oh, no!" Annie cried. "Don't do that! It's going to get—"

"Ruined!" Becca groaned as Bomber's paw

got caught in an eyehole. The cat pulled her paw out, tearing the hole and making it bigger.

"Sorry," Olmo said. "But it's okay." He put the head back on. "Rex just has one big eye, that's all."

"I guess it looks better that way," said Annie, trying hard to be patient. "More frightening. Anyway, I'll go get the audience."

"I don't want that," Gregory said.

"Not again," said Annie. "All right, we'll vote on it!" She stared at Becca and Olmo. "All in favor of having an audience, raise your hand. By the way, the audience is going to be my mother, and she's baking some cookies for us."

Olmo's hand shot up. "I vote yes."

"Me, too," said Becca. "Mrs. K. makes the best cookies."

Annie looked at Gregory.

"All right," he said reluctantly.

"Yippee!" said Annie. "I'll go get Mom. Maybe my dad can come, too."

A few moments later she came back alone.

"My mom is putting in the geraniums,"

Annie said with a disappointed look on her face. "My dad is busy writing. He has a deadline. And the cookies are still in the oven."

"That's okay," said Becca. "We can pretend."

"It won't be the same," said Annie. "We've done a lot of work on the play. I want to see if people like it."

"Maybe we can show them at our next dress rehearsal," said Olmo. "Maybe we should just keep practicing by ourselves." He put on his costume.

"You're right," said Annie. "Maybe we'll get an audience another time." She smiled at all three of them. "Since nobody's watching, let's start in the middle," she said cheerfully. "Let's start at the part where Rex has a fight with the evil mad duchess."

"Mokay," Olmo mumbled from under his head. "I mike dat mart."

"You have to speak louder when you're wearing your dino head!" Annie yelled. "Otherwise we won't understand you!"

"Okay!" Olmo yelled back. "I like that part!"

Annie took her spot behind the pine tree. Gregory and Becca knelt down on the ground, while Olmo stood in front of them. Annie darted out from behind the tree.

"Ra-ta-tu-ee!" cried Olmo. "Stay away from my children! You are an evil mad duchess from outer space."

Annie glared. "Out of my way, you old-fashioned string-bean lizard!"

"Rrrrr!" Olmo roared. "I will eat you!"

"Not if I smash you with a meteor!" Annie cried. Suddenly Annie felt a tapping on her shoulder. It was Gregory.

"What do you want?" Annie said. "You're interrupting the play."

"There's someone out there," Gregory said softly.

"Out where?" said Annie impatiently.

"Out there," Gregory pointed. "There's someone watching us."

Annie looked at the edge of the circle. Someone was sitting on the ground watching them. Someone she'd never seen before.

It was the audience!

Chapter Four

The Little Mystery

The girl in the lawn chair was very small, with large, brown eyes and short, brown hair. She stared at them. Annie, Becca, Gregory, and Olmo stared back.

"Unicorns!" the stranger said.

"No, not unicorns," Annie said, walking across the circle to her. "Dinosaurs. We're putting on a dinosaur play. Do you like it?"

The girl nodded.

"Who is she?" said Becca.

"She's a baby," said Olmo.

"I am *not* a baby," said the girl. "I'm four. The play is very excitable."

"She means exciting," said Olmo.

"She uses big words for a little kid," said Becca.

"But where does she come from?" said Gregory.

"What's your name?" Annie asked the little girl.

"Georgia," she answered. "But sometimes I call myself Dorothy. But I know I'm not *really* Dorothy. If I were Dorothy, I would live in Kansas."

"But where do you live?" asked Annie.

Georgia blinked her eyes. "Actually," she said, "I'm not sure. Actually I'm lost."

"Lost?" said Gregory. "Oh, no!"

"Don't you know your address?" Annie asked Georgia.

"I used to know it," said Georgia, "but now I don't."

"You have to live somewhere!" said Olmo.

"Geor-gia . . . Geor-gia . . ." a woman's voice was calling through the woods.

31

Georgia jumped up and smiled. "It's my mommy!"

A woman in a jogging outfit stepped out of the trees. "Georgia!" she said. "There you are!"

"Hi, Mommy," Georgia said. "I got lost. I was watching a play about rhinos."

"Dinos," Annie corrected her. She turned to the woman. "She doesn't know her address."

"That's because we've just moved here from California," Georgia's mother explained.

Annie's mother appeared at the edge of the hideout. "Hi, everybody," she said. "The cookies are just about ready. Am I too late for the rehearsal?"

"No, Mom," said Annie. "You're just in time. This girl named Georgia got lost and here's her mother."

"I'm Ellie Grill," said Georgia's mother. "We've just moved in up the road. Your children were entertaining my daughter. She wandered out of our backyard."

"I'm Josie Kramer," said Annie's mother with a smile.

"We're rehearsing a play," Annie said to

Mrs. Grill. "Would you and Georgia like to watch?"

"How delightful," said Mrs. Grill.

"The play is very excitable," Georgia said, smiling.

"I'll go get the cookies and some lemonade," said Mrs. Kramer.

"Could you use some help?" asked Mrs. Grill.

"Sure," said Mrs. K.

The two mothers went into the house. Georgia ran over to Bomber and started playing with her. Olmo did a somersault and Becca sat down. Gregory walked over to the tire swing.

Annie had dragged over a lawn chair and was getting another one. "Hurry up!" she ordered. "Take your places! You sit down there," she directed Georgia.

"No," Georgia replied. "I want to be in the play."

"But you can't," said Annie. "You don't know what we're doing."

"We've been rehearsing," Becca explained. "We already know our lines."

"I'll write another play tomorrow," said Annie. "You can be in that one, all right?"

"She can be in this one," said Gregory. "She can take my place."

"She won't know what to do," said Annie. "*You* have to do it." She looked up as her mother and Mrs. Grill stepped out of the house. "Here they come!" she said nervously.

Becca and Olmo and Gregory put on their dinosaur heads. Annie's mother and Mrs. Grill sat down in the lawn chairs. Georgia curled up on the ground with Bomber.

"This is a play about dinosaurs," Annie announced, facing her audience. Her heart began to beat very fast. "I wrote it, but Becca, Olmo, and Gregory helped out, too. It's a play about how the dinosaurs get destroyed by a mad duchess—that's my part."

"Sounds interesting," Mrs. Grill said to Mrs. Kramer.

Annie swallowed. "We'll start at the part when the mad duchess is being surrounded by angry dinosaurs."

Annie looked at Olmo and Becca. They were in their places. Gregory was sitting on his

34

knees with his arms folded in front of him. He had taken his dinosaur head off.

Annie walked over to him. "Hurry up!" she hissed.

"I don't want to," Gregory said. "People are watching!"

"They're supposed to watch," said Annie. She felt very frustrated. It was silly of Gregory to be so shy. She picked up the cardboard box and shoved it onto his head.

"Rreech-ra! Rreech-ra!" cried Olmo, starting the scene.

"Trummy-tummy-boogy-bat!" said Becca.

Gregory stood up and screamed. "Acch!"

"Reggi-beggi-rop-top!" said Olmo.

"Roob-ti-diga-bye-top-too!" said Becca.

"Acch!" cried Gregory. "My tooth is lost!"

Annie looked at him. That line was not in the script!

"My tooth!" he cried again, taking off his dino head.

Olmo and Becca took off their heads, too. "Did your tooth fall out?" asked Becca. "That's great!"

"It's not great," said Gregory. "I lost it. I mean . . . it's nowhere!"

Mrs. Kramer and Mrs. Grill stood up. So did Georgia and Bomber. The dino heads were scattered everywhere.

"Oh, no," Annie muttered. "Why did you have to lose your tooth in the middle of the play?"

"I didn't," said Gregory. "You knocked it out!"

"Knocked it out?" said Annie. "I did not!"

Becca and Olmo got down on their hands and knees and began looking for Gregory's tooth in the grass and leaves. Mrs. Kramer looked in Gregory's pants cuffs.

Gregory looked like he was going to cry. "I saved that tooth for a long time in my mouth," he said. "I felt it with my tongue just a minute ago."

"I didn't knock it out," Annie insisted. "I'm sorry your tooth is missing. But it's not my fault."

"I didn't want to wear that dino head," Gregory said. "You pushed it onto my head, and then my tooth was *gone*. You knocked it out!"

"No, I didn't!" said Annie. "I was just helping you put on your costume!"

Mrs. Kramer sighed. "I'm sorry, Gregory. I can't seem to find your tooth."

"A tooth is so tiny," Mrs. Grill agreed sadly. "It's like finding a needle in a haystack."

Gregory's lip quivered. "You mean it's lost forever?"

"Maybe if we keep looking, we'll find it," said Becca.

But Gregory was already walking off toward his house. Annie followed quickly behind him. "Where are you going?" she cried.

"Home," Gregory said, not looking back at her.

Chapter
Five

Annie and Gregory

"That Gregory is so stubborn!" Annie said to Becca. The two girls were staring at the red-brick house. "It's been three days and he hasn't come out yet."

"He has, too," Becca said.

Annie looked at her. "How do you know that?"

Becca walked over to an old tree and pointed to a hole in the trunk. "Look in there," she said.

Annie looked. Inside the hole was a bat— Gregory's bat!

"See," said Becca. "He has come out. He just won't come out when we're here."

Annie sighed. "He's still mad at us."

"He's not mad at us," Becca corrected her. "He's mad at *you!*"

Annie looked down at the ground. "I know."

The girls heard a loud noise in the trees. It was Olmo, charging through on his bicycle. "Hi!" he said. "I took the shortcut. Has Gregory been here?"

Becca shook her head. "Not while we've been here."

They heard music coming from the woods, then a small voice singing "Over the Rainbow." Soon Georgia appeared in the hideout.

"Hi, Georgia!" Becca said brightly.

"How did you get here?" Annie asked, lifting an eyebrow.

"Mommy let me go on the path again all by myself," Georgia said proudly. "It's like the yellow brick road."

Annie peered through the trees. Mrs. Grill was at the top of the path, waving.

"Well," said Becca, "everyone's here. Everyone except Gregory."

"Yes, he is!" Georgia sang out. She pointed to the red-brick house. Gregory was peeking out from one of the windows.

"There he is!" said Olmo. "Hey, Gregory!"

Gregory looked at Olmo, Becca, and Georgia. Then he looked at Annie and disappeared from the window.

"He keeps doing that!" said Annie. "He's always peeking. I'm beginning to think he's a spy."

"No, he's not," said Becca. "I don't think so."

"Neither do I," said Olmo.

"Me neither," said Georgia.

"Then why does he keep doing that?" said Annie. Everyone looked at her. "I know what you're thinking," said Annie. "I already told Gregory that I was sorry. It didn't make any difference."

"That's because he's still mad," said Becca. "I would be, too, if I'd missed the tooth fairy."

Annie sat down on the ground. She rested her back against the big pine tree. "I know what!" she said. "I'll write a new play! He'll have a part where he won't be a dino. Then he'll come out and play with us."

"Good idea," said Olmo.

Annie wrote a note in her notebook.

Annie tore out the page, folded the note, and put it into the tree hole. "There!" she said. "That's for Gregory."

"Do you think he'll read it?" said Becca. "What does it say?"

"It's an invitation," said Annie.

"An invitation!" cried Georgia. "To a birthday party?"

"It's not for a party," said Annie. "It's for a play." She looked up at the red-brick house again. Gregory was at the window. She knew he had seen her put the note in the tree hole. Now she had to wait for his answer.

Early the next day, Annie checked the tree

Dear Gregory,
    This is an invitation to be in my new play. I am writing it just for you. I promise you will not be a dino. This time you will have a very good part that you will like.
        From
        Annie

hole. The invitation was gone. She climbed the steps to Gregory's porch and knocked on the door. Gregory's mother opened it up.

"Hi, Mrs. Denton," said Annie.

"Hi, Annie," Mrs. Denton said with a smile. "How are you?"

"Okay, I guess," Annie answered. "Can Gregory come out?"

"He's in the family room," his mother replied. "I'll tell him you're here."

Annie waited on the porch until Gregory came outside.

"Hi," he said.

"Hi," said Annie.

Gregory looked down. "Did you really write a whole play just for me?"

Annie blushed. "Yes, I wrote it last night. I worked very hard on it. I wanted you to know how sorry I am. About . . . knocking your tooth out."

"Oh," said Gregory. "That's okay."

Annie looked at him. "Will you be in the new play, then? It's very interesting. You have the starring part."

"What is it?" asked Gregory.

"It's the part of a gardener who becomes an archaeologist. You will develop an interest in paleontology," Annie said proudly.

Annie thought Gregory looked interested.

"Will people be watching?" he asked after a moment.

"Not at first," Annie said. "But maybe after we've rehearsed for a long time."

"I still don't think I want to be in it, though," said Gregory. "I just don't like acting."

"All right," said Annie. "We'll put on the play for you then."

Gregory smiled. Annie saw the space where Gregory's tooth used to be.

"That's a big hole in your mouth," she said.

"It was a big tooth," said Gregory.

"Too bad we couldn't find it," said Annie.

Gregory nodded. "Maybe an animal took it."

"Maybe a dog ate it," Annie suggested. "Or a squirrel."

Gregory chuckled. "Or maybe Bomber."

Annie's eyes opened wide. "I hope not! Anyway, are you still mad at me?"

Gregory shrugged. "No."

"My mom says I'm bossy," Annie confided.

"You're not bossy!" said Gregory. "You're smart!"

"You think so?" said Annie. "Thanks a lot! Come on—let's go to the hideout! I want to show you something."

Annie led Gregory to a spot on the ground that was marked with three pebbles. It was just to the left of the pine tree.

"There's something buried there," Annie whispered.

Gregory looked at the three pebbles. "What?"

"Something for my new play," said Annie. "A fossil."

"A fossil?" asked Gregory. "A real one?"

"No," said Annie. "A pretend fossil. It's the dino head I made for you."

Gregory looked puzzled. "You buried that?"

"Yes," said Annie. "It's my surprise ending. At the end of the play, we'll dig it up."

"Wow," said Gregory. "That sounds neat."

He stood up. "You must have dug a very deep hole."

"Not too deep," Annie said. "I flattened the box out."

"Oh," said Gregory. "I didn't see you."

Annie smiled. "I know you didn't. I made sure you weren't at the window."

Gregory laughed. "Did you tell everybody else about the fossil?"

"No," said Annie. "You're the only one who knows. It has to be a secret. So don't tell."

"I won't," said Gregory.

They climbed up into the treehouse. "I'm sorry about the tooth fairy," said Annie.

"That's okay," Gregory said. "The tooth fairy's pretty smart. She came anyway."

"Hey!" Gregory leaned out of the tree. "I see Becca walking down the road. She's got Georgia with her!"

"And here comes Olmo on his bike!" added Annie.

"Hey, Gregory," Annie said.

Gregory looked at her.

"I'm glad you moved in," said Annie.

"In where?" Gregory asked.

Annie pointed to the red-brick house. "In there—next door to me. In Nan—" She stopped herself. She'd been about to say in Nancy McBride's house. But it wasn't her old friend's house anymore. It was her new friend Gregory's house.

Chapter Six

The Play Goes On

The next evening, Annie put on the new play she had written for Gregory. Becca, Olmo, and Georgia each had a part. They had been rehearsing the play the whole day. They were going to have a large audience.

"So far there are eight people," Annie whispered, peeking out through the trees.

"Are my mom and dad here yet?" asked Olmo.

"Yes, they're here," said Becca. "I can see them."

"I see my mommy, too," said Georgia.

"Here comes Gregory," Annie said. She watched Gregory take a seat in the front row. "His parents and sister are with him."

Annie's dad came backstage.

"Hi, kids," he said with a smile.

Olmo and Georgia smiled back at him. "Hi, Mr. K.," said Becca.

"Did you and Mom put out the refreshments for after the show?" Annie wanted to know.

Her dad nodded. "Just like you told us to. Lemonade, brownies, and watermelon."

"Great," said Annie. "Everything's set."

"Everything except Bomber," said Mr. Kramer. "She's tearing around all over the place."

"Annie let me give her some catnip," said Olmo.

"Should I put her in the house?" Mr. Kramer asked Annie. "She might disturb the play."

"That's okay," said Annie. "Bomber can't wreck anything. Besides, she's our usher."

Annie's dad patted Annie on the shoulder. "Ready to start the show?"

Annie gulped. "I guess. I'll just check the props." Dashing out onto the grassy circle, she checked the gardening tools she'd borrowed from her mother. They were just where she'd left them. And the pebbles next to the pine tree were there, too. Annie smiled. Olmo, Becca, and Georgia knew she had buried a fossil, but they didn't know where! The only ones who knew that were Annie and Gregory.

"Ready, Annie dear?" Mrs. Kramer called from her seat.

"Ready, Mom," Annie answered.

Annie ran backstage into the trees. She had never been so excited in her life. "It's time to start," she told the actors.

"Do our costumes look all right?" Becca asked nervously. Becca was wearing a man's hat, Olmo had on a big white bandage, and Georgia was wearing a wreath of flowers. Annie had on a sun visor.

"We look great!" said Annie. "Let's go!"

They ran onto the stage and began the play. Becca was the evil head of a museum. Annie was the narrator—and also the gardener. That was the part she had written for Gregory.

51

The gardener was actually an archaeologist who became an expert in paleontology after digging up the bone of a dinosaur.

At first the play went very well. Becca sent Annie out to find some fossils. She found a mummy who moved, played by Olmo. Then she found an ancient statue who sang, played by Georgia. Everyone, including Georgia, remembered their lines.

Finally it was time for Annie's big scene. The head of the museum was telling her to go out and find a fossil—the bone of a dinosaur. Georgia and Olmo would be going with her.

Annie's heart beat faster and faster. This was her favorite part of the play—the surprise ending! This was when they'd dig up the dino head she had buried earlier.

Suddenly Bomber came flying out of nowhere. The cat tore across the stage and raced toward the pine tree. She whipped around the tree, then ran back toward center stage.

"Hey, what's that cat doing on stage?" Olmo's father said with a laugh.

"Bomber's stealing the show!" Gregory's dad chuckled.

"Maybe she sees a squirrel," said Mrs. Kramer.

Annie felt terrible. Everyone was paying attention to Bomber. Her cat was interrupting the show. "Get off the stage," Annie said. She scooped up the rambunctious cat and gave her to Mr. Kramer. Then passing the pine tree, she glanced on the ground for the pebbles. Bomber had knocked them away!

"Let's go find a dino bone," Olmo said, getting on with the play. He walked stiffly as if he were a mummy.

"Yes, let's find a dino bone," said Georgia. She struck a pose as if she were a statue.

Annie passed out some gardening tools. "Why don't you two help me?" she said. "We'll dig . . ." Without the pebbles to mark the spot, she'd have to guess where to start digging. She felt very excited and nervous. She knew the fossil was next to the pine tree, but suddenly she couldn't remember on which side, the right or the left.

She walked to the right of the tree. "We'll dig here," she said, pointing to a spot on the ground. She took a quick look at Gregory.

Maybe he remembered where the fossil was buried. But he couldn't help her sitting out in the audience.

Olmo, Georgia, and Annie began digging. They dug for a very long time.

"There's nothing in here, Annie," Georgia whimpered.

"I thought you said you buried something," Olmo chimed in.

"What's wrong?" Becca whispered, tiptoeing over. "Did you forget where you hid it?"

The audience began to move around in their seats.

"Is the play over?" Annie heard someone whisper.

Annie felt like crying. She couldn't find the fossil. She would have to call off the play. The whole thing was going to be ruined.

Suddenly Gregory got up from his chair. He grabbed a trowel and ran toward the tree.

"How about this spot?" he said loudly.

"Hi, Gregory," said Georgia. "Who are you?"

"I am a gardener," said Gregory, looking straight out at the audience. "A gardener who is really an archaeologist. And I have recently developed an interest in paleontology."

Annie sighed with relief, then she smiled. Not only did Gregory seem to remember where the fossil was hidden, he seemed to be having a good time. "A gardener who is an archaeologist and a paleontologist?" she said brightly. "That's just what we need! Let's dig where he tells us!"

Gregory stuck his trowel into the dirt, in a spot just to the left of the pine tree. Soon everyone else was digging along with him.

Olmo was the first to discover it. "I hit something!" he yelled. "We found it! A real dinosaur bone!" He pointed to the flattened-out box.

"It's a dino head!" Georgia giggled.

Gregory laughed. "It used to be mine!"

Olmo grinned and raised the box above his shoulders. "Ouch!" he said as something small, white, and hard bounced onto his nose and dropped to the ground. "What was that?"

Gregory got down on his knees to look. "It's my tooth!" he cried happily.

"Wow!" said Annie. "You found it."

"It was in the box," said Becca. "It was probably caught inside the flap."

"This is great," Olmo exclaimed. "Now Gregory will get his five dollars!"

"What's going on?" Mr. Kramer asked from the audience. "What's happening? Is the play over?"

"Not yet," Annie said. "We found a tooth!"

"It's Gregory's," Olmo yelled. "The tooth fairy is going to give him five dollars!"

"Five dollars, eh?" said Gregory's dad from the audience.

Georgia's mother laughed. "That must be a pretty rich tooth fairy!"

Everyone in the audience laughed. But Annie was very serious. She wanted to go on with the play.

"It's a dino tooth!" she yelled loudly. She stared at everyone until they quieted down. "We found a real fossil. Let's take it back to the museum!"

"To the museum," said Olmo. "Let's go!"

"Let's go!" said Georgia.

"Let's go!" said Gregory. "To the museum!"

They carried the dino tooth back to the museum and gave it to Becca. Then they said the rest of their lines.

"Bravo!" cried Mr. Kramer when the play was over. He had stood up and was clapping loudly.

Everyone else in the audience was clapping, too.

"Thanks for saving me," Annie whispered to Gregory.

"That's okay." Gregory smiled. "I'm going to get five dollars."

"Hey, kids!" called Mr. Kramer. "Take a bow!"

Annie blushed. She grabbed Olmo's and Becca's hands. Becca held Georgia's hand, and Olmo held Gregory's.

"I like this play!" Olmo said loudly.

"It was almost like a fairy tale!" Becca exclaimed.

"Let's do another one!" said Georgia.

Annie felt very happy. She could hardly believe that one of her plays had really gone on. She'd written it and rehearsed it, and gotten

an audience. Not only that, it was a hit and she and her friends had had fun. She wanted to put on more and more plays.

The players bowed deeply. The audience was still clapping. Bomber came onto the stage and everyone laughed.

Then they all had brownies and water-melon. They gave Bomber some lemonade and she liked it.

Everybody agreed they had had a wonderful time.

And that was the start of Annie K.'s Theater.

Annie K.'s Play
THE DINOSAUR TOOTH

If you enjoyed Annie K.'s play, you, too, can put on THE DINOSAUR TOOTH. All you need is four or five friends, some clothing and supplies you'll find around the house, and some after-school or vacation time. Have fun!

Cast

The Narrator
The Gardener
The Head of the Museum
The Mummy
The Singing Statue
The Dinosaur
The Photographer

These parts can be played by either boys or girls. If there are not enough actors for all the parts, the same person who plays the Dinosaur may play the role of the Photographer in the first section of the play. In the last section, the Narrator may play this part.

Set

The play begins in the office of the museum. Later on it takes place in a swamp. The only thing on stage is a tree. This does not have to be a real tree—it can be a chair or a box that the actors pretend is a tree.

Props

Forks, knives, and spoons to be used as digging tools.

A dinosaur tooth—you can use a skinny white stone, a piece of painted wood, or a clay model made into a tooth shape. The tooth should be long enough to tie a piece of cord or twine to.

A knapsack in which the Gardener carries tools.

A map and a pillow.

Costumes

Whatever you think your character might be wearing; the person who plays the Dinosaur may or may not want to wear a "dinosaur head." You can make such a head out of a cardboard box with cut eyeholes and a cut-out mouth. The box can then be painted brownish or green with cardboard plates or horns added depending on the type of dinosaur you'd like to be. The person who plays the Head of the Museum might like to wear a witch cape.

A man's hat, a large white bandage, a wreath of flowers, a sun visor.

NARRATOR
(Speaking to the audience) Hi! The name of this play is *The Dinosaur Tooth*. Once upon a time, there was a lowly gardener. The gardener worked in a museum.

GARDENER
Hi, I'm the gardener. I work in the museum. (The Gardener starts digging around the tree.)

NARRATOR
You might think that a museum is an odd place for a gardener to work, but the lobby of the museum had lots of plants. Somebody had to take care of them. But the gardener did not like her job. She wanted to be an archaeologist.

GARDENER
I want to work inside the museum. I want to take care of things that are old.

NARRATOR
One day, the gardener saw the head of the museum.

GARDENER
Please, sir— (She follows the Head of the Museum into his office.)

HEAD OF THE MUSEUM
Who are you?

GARDENER
I'm the gardener. I take care of the plants. But I really want to work inside the museum. I want to take care of statues and mummies.

HEAD OF THE MUSEUM
You silly gardener. In order to work in my museum, you must do something great, like I did.

GARDENER
Like what?

HEAD OF THE MUSEUM
Go dig up something! Go dig up something old.

GARDENER
All right. I'll do it! (She picks up her knapsack and leaves.)

HEAD OF THE MUSEUM
Ha, ha! She'll never do it. She's only a dunce of a gardener.

NARRATOR
The gardener went to Egypt.

GARDENER
(Starting to dig) This looks like a good spot.

NARRATOR
She dug and dug and dug until she found a mummy.

(The Mummy lies down at the Gardener's feet.)

GARDENER
What a wonderful mummy! And I found it!

NARRATOR
She took the mummy back to the museum.

(The Narrator helps the Gardener carry the Mummy back to the museum. They stand the Mummy up straight. The Mummy is very still.)

GARDENER
(To the Head of the Museum) Look! I found a mummy. Now, can I work *inside* the museum?

HEAD OF THE MUSEUM
No. Stay out there in the lobby!

NARRATOR
The head of the museum was mean and dishonest. He went to the phone and called up the newspaper.

HEAD OF THE MUSEUM
(On the telephone) Get over to the museum. I've made an important discovery.

NARRATOR
He got his picture taken and was in all of the newspapers.

PHOTOGRAPHER
Smile please.

(The Head of the Museum poses for a picture with the Mummy; the Photographer snaps it.)

GARDENER
Hey! *You* didn't dig up that mummy! *I* did!

HEAD OF THE MUSEUM
Ha, ha. Nobody in the world knows that but you.

GARDENER
Won't you at least let me take care of it? It is my mummy.

HEAD OF THE MUSEUM
(Slyly) Perhaps . . . if you'll go dig up something else. Perhaps an old statue.

NARRATOR
So the gardener went to Greece and dug up an ancient statue.

(The Gardener starts to dig. The Statue comes and stands in front of her.)

GARDENER
An old statue! It's beautiful!

NARRATOR

She took the statue back to the museum and showed it to the head of the museum.

(The Narrator helps the Gardener carry the Statue back to the museum.)

GARDENER

Look what I found!

HEAD OF THE MUSEUM

Very interesting. It's quite old. Just what I need for the museum.

GARDENER

Can I have a job inside, taking care of it?

HEAD OF THE MUSEUM

Not yet. You stay out in the lobby.

NARRATOR

The head of the museum called the newspapers again.

HEAD OF THE MUSEUM
(On the telephone) Get over here. I've made another discovery.

NARRATOR
He got his picture taken with the statue.

(The Head of the Museum poses with the Statue.)

PHOTOGRAPHER
(Taking their picture) Smile please! (He exits.)

GARDENER
You're mean.

HEAD OF THE MUSEUM
(Slyly) No, I'm not. I'll tell you what—if you make one more discovery, I'll give you a job inside the museum. You'll get to take care of your mummy and statue.

GARDENER
(Very excited) What do I have to do?

HEAD OF THE MUSEUM
Go find me the tooth of a dinosaur.

GARDENER
A dinosaur tooth? I have always been interested in paleontology. But where can I find it?

HEAD OF THE MUSEUM
In Mosquito Swamp. (He takes out a map.) Here's a map.

GARDENER
(Picking up her knapsack) Thanks a lot. I'll bring back the tooth.

HEAD OF THE MUSEUM
(Waving) Good-bye.

NARRATOR
The head of the museum was very sneaky. He had sent the gardener to Mosquito Swamp to get rid of her. He was afraid she would tell the world that he was a liar.

HEAD OF THE MUSEUM

She'll never find a dinosaur tooth in that swamp, ha, ha. The only thing she'll find is the mysterious monster Thunderfoot. Thunderfoot will eat her alive.

NARRATOR

Before the gardener left for the swamp, she sneaked inside the museum. She wanted to say good-bye to her mummy and statue.

GARDENER

Good-bye.

MUMMY

Where are you going?

GARDENER

To find the tooth of a dinosaur. Hey! You talk.

MUMMY

I move, too. (He does a cartwheel.)

STATUE

So do I. (She changes poses.) And I can sing "Frère Jacques." Frère Jacques, Frère Jacques . . .

MUMMY

Take us with you.

GARDENER

(Very happy) Okay. Let's go.

NARRATOR

They found their way to Mosquito Swamp.

MUMMY

Let's dig here.

(The Gardener, the Mummy, and the Statue start digging. The Dinosaur enters and stands behind the tree. The other three do not see him.)

DINOSAUR

Acch! Acch!

GARDENER

Did you hear something?

MUMMY

Yes. It sounded like a monster.

(The Dinosaur steps out from behind the tree.)

GARDENER

It *is* a monster! Run for your life!

(The Dinosaur chases them around and around the tree.)

DINOSAUR

Acch! Acch! Reega-reega. Tooth! Tooth!

(Suddenly the Dinosaur stops and falls down.)

GARDENER

(Stopping also) Hey, what's wrong with it?

STATUE

It looks sick. What kind of monster is this, anyway?

GARDENER

Now that I'm up close, it doesn't look like a monster. You know what it looks like? A dinosaur!

MUMMY

But the dinosaurs are all dead.

DINOSAUR
Acch! Acch! Reega-dino! Tooth! Tooth!

STATUE
He's trying to tell us something.

DINOSAUR
Reega-dino! Tooth!

GARDENER
I wish I knew dinosaur language.

NARRATOR
(Walking over) I do. He says that he's the last living dinosaur.

GARDENER
The last living dinosaur!

NARRATOR
And that he's got a toothache.

GARDENER
(Getting twine out of his knapsack) Tell him that I'll help him with his tooth. I'll pull it out for him.

(The Dinosaur nods as if he understands.)

NARRATOR
He understands you. He wants you to pull his tooth out.

GARDENER
Great! (She gives one end of the twine to the Mummy.) Here, you take one end of the string and I'll tie the other one to his tooth. (The Narrator helps the Gardener walk the Dino to a spot behind the tree. The Gardener then pretends to tie the other end of twine to the Dinosaur's tooth. Actually, the actor who is playing the Dinosaur should hold the end of the twine in his hand. While the Gardener and the Mummy and the Statue are getting ready to pull the tooth, the actor should tie the dinosaur tooth prop onto the end of the twine he is holding. The actor should try to do this without the audience seeing him.)

GARDENER
(Holding the other end of the twine along with the Mummy and the Statue) Okay, on the count of three, let's pull!

(To the Mummy and Statue) Ready?

MUMMY AND STATUE
Ready.

GARDENER
All right. One . . . two . . . three! (They pull on their end of the twine.)

(The actor playing the Dinosaur lets go of his end of the twine. The dinosaur tooth comes flying out onto the stage.)

DINOSAUR
Acch! Acch! Reega . . . Oh, oh, oh . . . (As if he is feeling better)

GARDENER
Look! A real dinosaur tooth! I can take it back to the museum! Let's go! (To the Dinosaur) Thanks a lot for letting me pull your tooth out!

DINOSAUR
Doog-da! Doog-da!

NARRATOR

The dino says wait!

GARDENER

What is it?

DINOSAUR

Doog-da piggy.

NARRATOR

He says he wants to go with you.

GARDENER

To the museum? Why not? He'll be the greatest discovery of all! I'll build a big cage for him.

NARRATOR

So they all went back to the museum.

(The four of them walk in a procession back to the museum, with the Gardener in the lead.)

GARDENER

(To the Mummy, Statue, and Dino) Wait here for a minute. (She walks over by herself and taps the Head of the Museum on the shoulder.) Hi!

HEAD OF THE MUSEUM
You're back! That's impossible.

GARDENER
No it isn't. Not only that, I found the tooth of a dinosaur. (She takes the tooth out of her knapsack.)

HEAD OF THE MUSEUM
You can't fool me. This isn't real.

GARDENER
Yes it is.

HEAD OF THE MUSEUM
Prove it.

GARDENER
Okay. (To the Dinosaur) Can you come here for a minute!

(The Dinosaur walks over, followed by the Mummy and Statue.)

HEAD OF THE MUSEUM
(Terrified) It's the monster! It's Thunderfoot!

GARDENER

No it's not. He's the last living dinosaur.

HEAD OF THE MUSEUM

The last living dinosaur? Is he friendly?

GARDENER

He's been friendly to us.

HEAD OF THE MUSEUM

Nice dino. (Petting the Dinosaur) You stay right there. (To the Gardener) Get out of my office. Take that mummy and statue back where they belong.

GARDENER

What are you going to do?

HEAD OF THE MUSEUM

I'm going to call the newspaper. This is the biggest discovery of all time.

GARDENER

And it's *my* discovery.

HEAD OF THE MUSEUM

Your discovery? Who would believe that a lowly gardener could discover the last living dinosaur?

MUMMY

I believe it.

STATUE

I believe it, too.

DINOSAUR

(Making loud, angry noises) Reeg-ra! Reeg-ra! Poot-toot-piggy!

HEAD OF THE MUSEUM

(Scared) What's he saying?

NARRATOR

He says dinos hate liars.

DINOSAUR

Reech-ra! Reech-ra! (Chasing the Head of the Museum)

NARRATOR

He says that he's going to eat you alive!

HEAD OF THE MUSEUM

(Terrified; running away from the Dino) Let me out of here!

DINOSAUR

(Chasing the Head of the Museum away) Reech-ra! Reech-ra!

MUMMY AND STATUE

Hooray!

NARRATOR

Terrified to show his face, the evil head of the museum was never heard of again. Photographers came and took pictures of the gardener and all her discoveries!

PHOTOGRAPHER

Smile please!

(The Gardener, Mummy, Statue, and Dinosaur pose together. The Photographer snaps their picture.)

NARRATOR

The gardener was made the new head of the museum. She took good care of the mummy and statue.

(The Gardener leads the Mummy and Statue to their spots.)

And she built a cage for the last living dinosaur.

(The Gardener leads the Dinosaur to his spot and pets him.)

And she put the dinosaur tooth in a very special place.

(Carrying the dinosaur tooth on a pillow, the Gardener puts it down next to the Dinosaur.)

And they all lived happily ever after!

STATUE

(Singing happily) Frère Jacques, Frère Jacques . . .

DINOSAUR

Reech-ra! Reech-ra!

MUMMY
(Doing a cartwheel) The end!

(Actors take a bow)

ABOUT THE AUTHOR

SHARON DENNIS WYETH has written a number of books for young readers, among them a series called Pen Pals. She is also a playwright and has written for television. She lives with her husband and daughter in New York City.

ABOUT THE ILLUSTRATOR

HEIDI PETACH lives in Cincinnati, Ohio, with her husband and son as well as a dog, a bird, two snails, and a frog. She has written and/or illustrated more than two dozen books for young readers. In addition, she has a master's degree in music from Indiana University and has written commissioned symphonic works.

GIRL DETECTIVES
HAVE MORE FUN!

Taffy Sinclair is perfectly gorgeous and totally stuck-up. Ask her rival Jana Morgan or anyone else in the sixth grade of Mark Twain Elementary. Once you meet Taffy, life will **never** be the same.

Don't Miss Any of the Terrific Taffy Sinclair Titles from Betsy Haynes!

Follow the adventures of Jana and the rest of **THE FABULOUS FIVE** in a new series by Betsy Haynes.

Great FREE offer
just for you!

Join SNEAK PEEKS™!

Do you want to know what's new before anyone else? Do you like to read great books about girls just like you? If you do, then you won't want to miss SNEAK PEEKS™! Be the first of your friends to know what's hot ... When you join SNEAK PEEKS™, we'll send you FREE inside information in the mail about the latest books ... *before they're published!* Plus updates on your favorite series, authors, and exciting new stories filled with friendship and fun ... adventure and mystery ... girlfriends and boyfriends.

It's easy to be a member of SNEAK PEEKS™. Just fill out the coupon below ... and get ready for fun! It's FREE! Don't delay—sign up today!

Mail to: SNEAK PEEKS™,
Bantam Books, P.O. Box 1011,
South Holland, IL 60473

☐ YES! I want to be a member of Bantam's SNEAK PEEKS™ and receive hot-off-the-press information in the mail.

Name _____ Birthdate _____

Address _____

City/State _____ Zip _____

SK31—10/89